MOMMY'S HOMETOWN

To my parents
HL

For Aunt Connie
JK

Text copyright © 2022 by Hope Lim
Illustrations copyright © 2022 by Jaime Kim

First edition 2022

Library of Congress Catalog Card Number pending
ISBN 978-1-5362-1332-4

22 23 24 25 26 27 APS 10 9 8 7 6 5 4 3 2 1

Printed in Humen, Dongguan, China

This book was typeset in Agenda Medium.
The illustrations were created digitally.

Candlewick Press
99 Dover Street
Somerville, Massachusetts 02144

www.candlewick.com

MOMMY'S HOMETOWN

Hope Lim

illustrated by Jaime Kim

CANDLEWICK PRESS

At night, Mommy would tell me about where she grew up.

She said an old river weaved through her village
like a long thread.
It sparkled in the morning and shimmered at dusk.

She and her friends would walk to the river and play there all day.

They caught fish,

splashed each other,

unearthed treasures
beneath rocks,

and dried themselves on the pebbled riverbank.

The mountains nearby stood like giants.
The sky was filled with billowing clouds she could watch forever.

I have dreamed about playing in the river.
And tomorrow I am going to see it for myself.

But when we finally arrive in Mommy's hometown, it doesn't look the way I had imagined.
Mommy says over the years her village has grown into a big city.
The new replaced the old.

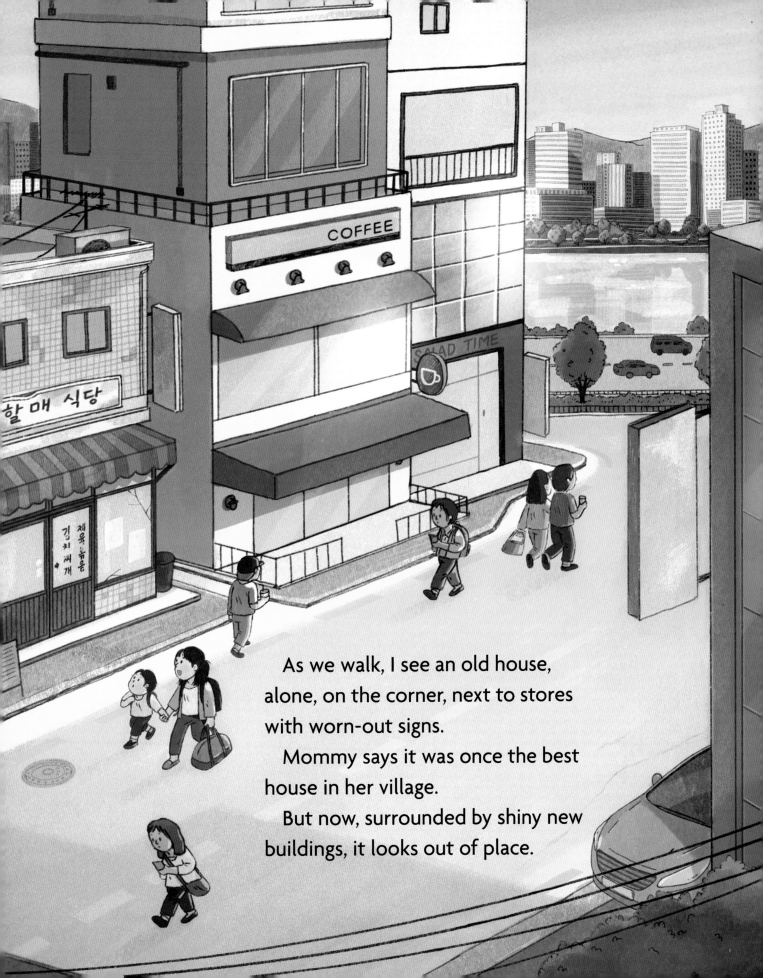

As we walk, I see an old house, alone, on the corner, next to stores with worn-out signs.

Mommy says it was once the best house in her village.

But now, surrounded by shiny new buildings, it looks out of place.

Is this really the same place where Mommy grew up? Everything is different from her stories.

Then we hear Grandma calling us.
Mommy smiles and says, "Some things change,
and some things stay the same."

Later that day, Mommy and I walk down the street toward the river.

She says the road to the river used to be all dirt with no cars.

I wish I could see what it was like back then.

Now, in place of mountains, tall apartment buildings stand like giants.
In place of billowing clouds, the gray sky spreads low.
In place of pebbled paths, concrete walkways line the river.
And no one splashes in the water.
But Mommy and I wade in.

The stream, cold and strong,
swirls against our legs.
   Hand in hand, we waddle
like two ducks through the
rushing water.

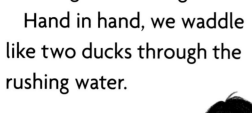

I jump when a school of
tiny fish darts by us.

With our backs bent and heads together,
we unearth treasures until our feet and
hands are icy cold.

While we wait for our feet to dry, I notice others gathering near the river.

"People still come here after work and school," Mommy says. "Over the years, so much has changed, but this river is just how I remember it."

On our way home, the sky glows
in soft hues as we walk through
the city.

The stores with worn-out signs are now open.
Even the old house is lit up, not lonely at all
but home to a family.

"I used to play on this street until the whole sky turned red and Grandma called me for dinner. Then I would race home."

I imagine Mommy playing as a girl under the red sky.
And I am there, too.

I hear Grandma calling us.

And we run home together.